read it yourself
PUSS IN BOOTS

All children have
a great ambition to read
to themselves . . .

and a sense of achievement when they can do so. The **read it yourself** *series has been devised to satisfy their ambition. Since many children learn from the Ladybird Key Words Reading Scheme, these stories have been based to a large extent on the Key Words List, and the tales chosen are those with which children are likely to be familiar.*

The series can of course be used as supplementary reading for any reading scheme. Puss in Boots *is intended for children reading up to Book 3c of the Ladybird Reading Scheme. The following words are additional to the vocabulary used at that level –*

Puss, his, master, or, boots, puts, my, bag, food, king, from, Marquis of Carrabas, partridges, eat, princess, marry, clothes, men, carriage, working, ogre, change, lion, mouse

Published by Ladybird Books Ltd Loughborough Leicestershire UK
Ladybird Books Inc Auburn Maine 04210 USA

Printed in England

Puss in Boots

by Fran Hunia
illustrated by Kathie Layfield

Ladybird Books

Here is Puss
with his master.

The boy has no Mummy
or Daddy.

He has no home.

I can help you

to get a home,

says Puss.

Get me some boots,

please.

Yes, says his master.

I can get some boots

for you.

He gets Puss

some red boots.

Puss puts the boots on.

I look good in my boots,

he says.

Please get me a bag, Master

His master gets Puss a bag.

The boy gives the bag to Puss.

Good, says Puss. I can have fun with this bag.

Puss puts some food
into the bag.

He puts it down.

A rabbit comes up
to the bag.

The rabbit sees the food.

It jumps into the bag
to get the food.

Puss gets the rabbit.

That is good, says Puss.

I have a rabbit.

I can give it to the king.

Puss sees the king.

He says, This rabbit

is from my master,

the Marquis of Carrabas.

The king is pleased.

He likes to eat rabbit.

Puss sees some partridges.

He says, I can get

some partridges for the king.

Puss puts some food

into his bag.

The partridges want the food

They go into the bag to get it

Puss gets the partridges.

Puss sees the king.

Here are some partridges

for you, he says.

They are from my master,

the Marquis of Carrabas.

Good, says the king.

I like partridges.

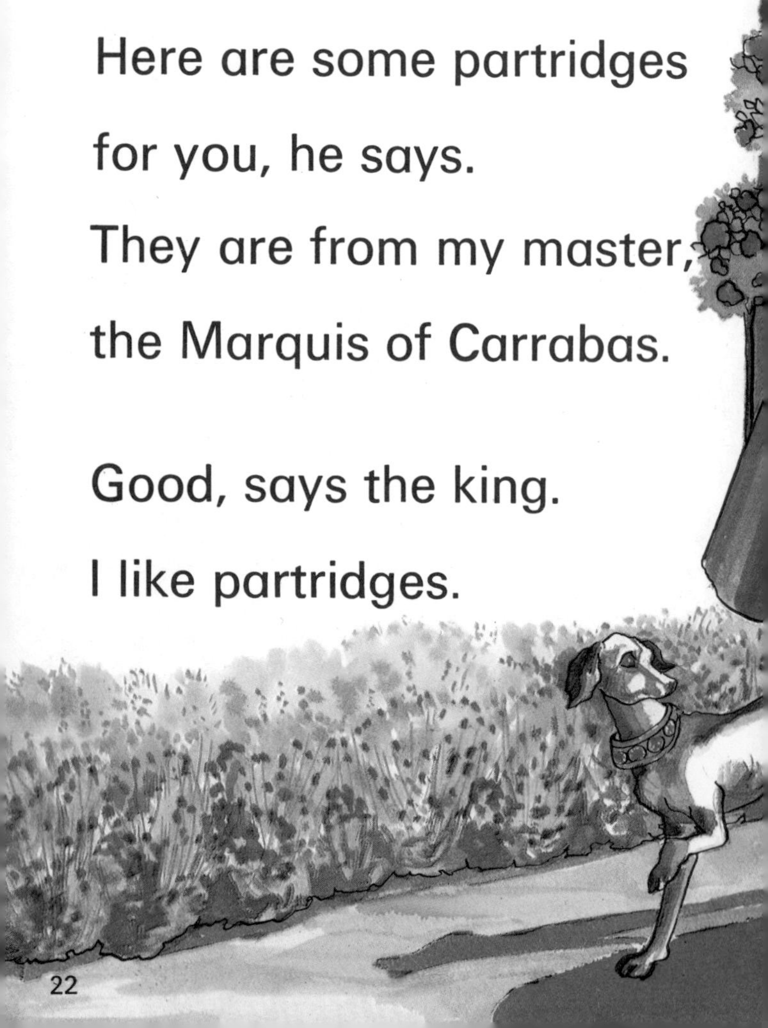

Puss is up in a tree.

He sees the king
and the princess.

He comes down
and says to his master,
Here come
the king and the princess.

Come with me,
and you can marry
the princess.

Get into the water,

says Puss.

His master jumps

into the water

with his clothes on.

The king and the princess come.

Puss says, Help, help!
The Marquis of Carrabas is in the water.
Please come and help my master!

The king's men help the boy.

They give the boy
some good clothes.

Please come with me,
says the king.

The boy gets
into the carriage
with the king
and the princess.

Puss sees some men working.

Here comes the king,

says Puss.

Please say you are working

for the Marquis of Carrabas.

Yes, say the men.

The king comes.

He sees the men working.

We are working

for the Marquis of Carrabas,

say the men.

That is good,

says the king.

Puss comes

to an ogre's home.

He says, Can I come in?

Yes, says the ogre.

(The ogre wants to eat Puss.)

Puss says to the ogre,

Can you change

into a lion?

Yes, says the ogre.

He changes into a lion.

That was good, says Puss

to the ogre.

Can you change

into a mouse?

Yes, says the ogre.

Look at me.

The ogre changes

into a mouse.

Puss jumps down.

He gets the mouse

and eats it.

The king comes.

Come in, says Puss.

This is my master's home.

It is a good home,

says the king.

Come in here and eat,

says Puss.

They go in and eat

the ogre's food.

Puss's master
likes the princess.

Please marry me,
he says.

Yes, says the princess.
I want to marry you.

The king is pleased.

Puss's master marries the princess.

Puss is pleased.

He likes the princess and the princess is good to Puss.